TAX and his friends

The first lessons on tax education for your children

Maria Claudia Hoepers

Praises

The little book on taxation by Maria Claudia Hoepers is an excellent resource designed to educate children and young people about "public power" through the instrument that supports any state structure: taxation.

The characters, who represent various aspects of the public administration and are anchored by the protagonist after whom the book is named, help children understand what administration entails, its costs, and its services to society, as well as its primary means of support.

The language is easily comprehensible, and the narrative is highly engaging for boys and girls as they learn about their responsibilities towards governmental powers and vice versa.

It truly is a primer on citizenship for the young.

The best way to prepare youth for the future is to instill virtues that make a good citizen, equip them with the simplicity to serve society, and explain clearly what the State is so that they feel a future responsibility towards their country.

I therefore congratulate Maria Claudia Hoepers on this initiative, which has been deemed successful by everyone in Brazil.

Dr. Ives Gandra da Silva Martins

Emeritus professor at the Universities of Mackenzie, UNIP, UNIFIEO, UNIFMU, CIEE/O, State of São Paulo, Military Command and General Staff Schools – ECEME, Superior War College –ESG, and the Judiciary of the Federal Regional Court – First Region; honorary professor at the Universities of Austral (Argentina), San Martin de Porres (Peru), and Vasili Goldis (Romania); doctor honoris causa from the Universities of Craiova (Romania) and from the PUCs-Paraná and RS, and chair professor at the University of Minho (Portugal); president of the Superior Council of Law at FECOMERCIO – SP; former president of the São Paulo Academy of Letters-APL and the Institute of Lawyers of São Paulo – IASP

Firstly, I'd like to say that we've decided to introduce tax education in our elementary school as soon as we heard about Maria Claudia Hoepers's life story, who dreamed of being happy and successful in school since childhood.

As time goes by, this dream turns into motivation and effort, and through her passion for education, children, and understanding of tax, an interesting book was born: *Tax And His Friends.*

By taking a closer look at the book, it's easier to notice that its context isn't only about tax education; it's much more than that. It brought to our fifth-grade students important knowledge about honesty, collaborative spirit, mother's wisdom, friendship, social behavior, and great citizenship lessons as well.

Secondly, in a joyful, friendly, and vibrantly colored way, tax education is developed, and the children learn it with pleasure, letting their imagination grow while enjoying learning with the characters of the story: Tax and his friends.

Among them, the little lion becomes an unforgettable and wise friend for all of them.

I strongly recommend the adoption of the book for every elementary school that has in its learning approaches the joy of having the school institution in every single child's heart, and the certainty that learning with pleasure is the key to happiness and success.

Adopting this book requires knowing that it is possible to learn about tax education with imagination and joy, both so present in this literature.

After reading and studying with Tax and his friends, our school's kids are ready to share their happiness and tax knowledge with others, because it was and will always be a learning memory to cherish.

I picture a world in which the same amazing experience for every kid is possible, in which every school can be a place with a positive environment where happiness leads to a better student performance.

To Tax and his friends, my loudest applause!

Arlete Steil Kumm
Principal of Colégio de Aplicação da Univali/Itajaí

I recommend reading *Tax and His Friends*, an educational book for children. It's an incredible work! Light, ethical, and fun! I really wish I had access to this when I was a child; it would have greatly helped in my adult life, without a doubt. I will keep this copy very dearly for Noah, my one-year-old son. When he learns to read, he will already have an advantage over his father, as he will start more well-informed and educated. I found the work incredible. Highly recommend! Happy reading to all!

Luigi Cani

Professional skydiver, eleven-time world record holder

Tax and His Friends is much more than literature; it is a true civic lesson for children (and perhaps adults) and should be mandatory reading for students in the latter stages of elementary school. My two children were fascinated by the work and interacted as I told them the story. This even helped them understand a bit more about my profession as a tax specialist and the importance of taxes. Congratulations to Maria Claudia Hoepers on her authorship, and may this book overcome all educational barriers, including geographical ones!

Letícia Mary Fernandes do Amaral

Business intelligence tax specialist, lawyer, vice president of IBPT, president of ABETRI, founder and CEO of IBPT LA Tax, Business & Education

---

Tax education for children? I must confess that at first, this idea made me quite thoughtful about how to tackle such a complex subject with fifth-grade students. However, with the help of the book Tax and His Friends, it was very enjoyable to carry out this project. The book uses language that is suitable for their age, with illustrations and a fantastic story.

As a teacher, my wish is for all students to have the opportunity to learn about taxes from an early age, so that they can become citizens capable of understanding the social function of taxation, recognizing the importance of monitoring the use of public resources, and motivated to exercise full citizenship.

Maraellen Pereira

Teacher

How do you explain what taxes are and how they impact our lives? If this topic is already dense and complex for adults, explaining it to my three curious young children was even more challenging.

The book, *Tax and His Friends* by Maria Claudia Hoepers, tackled the subject in a didactic, colorful, light, and fun way! Since then, my children love picking up receipts in stores to analyze them. They are shocked by the high tax amounts and always ask: how is the government going to use this money?

Priscila Rubbo Thá
Economist and mother of Sofia, Elisa, and Augusto

I really enjoy reading, and when I received the book, *Tax and His Friends*, I was delighted with the illustrations, its beautiful characters, and its easy-to-understand writing, talking about taxes in a fun way and their importance in society.

I hope there will soon be a continuation of this story so I can learn even more.

I thank the writer Maria Claudia for sharing with us.

Carolina Hoepers
Student, twelve years old

Tax education has always been a subject for adults, right? Those who think so are mistaken. In a playful and fun way, the book, Tax and His Friends, enables rich learning that allows children to understand the topic.

For the implementation of the Tax Education project, developed at CAU – UNIVALI Application School with fifth-grade students, this literary book was adopted. During the project, the classes engage in activities such as research, seminars, games, parodies, poems, and presentations, where the culmination occurs through a tax education fair, in which the students, with authority, present their discoveries.

Tax and His Friends is a book that allows for extremely important, necessary learning, and the children love tax education.

Kátia Campos
Educational advisor

Professor Maria Claudia, in her book, *Tax and His Friends*, manages to bring precise and responsible information about taxes, their necessity and the importance of their proper use, to children and other readers with a youthful spirit in a playful and enchanting way. It's an enjoyable read that reflects the concern of a true educator in teaching how to think, not what to think. Ultimately, it's a captivating read, with a storyline that engages the reader and fulfills the mission of responsible education about the role of taxes and the citizen.

Julberto Meira

University postgraduate professor, specialist in tax law, and master in business law and citizenship

---

The book, *Tax and His Friends*, presents us with a creative and engaging story, leading children and teachers along a fun path that culminates in the foundational knowledge of tax education. Investments, taxes, and duties become part of the daily discussions and conversations, involving and integrating children, families, and schools.

Lisiane Gazola Santos

Elementary years teacher – UNIVALI, professor and coordinator of the pedagogy course at the Lutheran University of Brazil (ULBRA)

Tax and His Friends really helped me to understand taxation. I had no idea how it worked, but now I look at the receipts from purchases and see how much tax is there. I also understand where all that money goes. The coolest part is that the characters really help to understand taxation and its benefits. Each character has a theme, but I liked Mother Cloud and Tax the most.

Camile Ferreira Leal Sabino

Student, fourteen years old

The book, *Tax and His Friends*, won me over. Maria Claudia had a bright idea—explaining how important and necessary taxes are in a playful and creative way. Involving children in this topic contributes to education and the building of a fairer and more conscious society. This is an amazing book. A work carried out with so much dedication by an incredible woman and professional. I believe that the book was the way in which Maria Claudia found to translate and realize her desire to educate and train. With love.

Monica Oliveira Camargo

Journalist

Seeing my daughter dive into this reading, which initially seemed so difficult for her to understand, was incredible. After all, understanding taxation seems to belong only to the adult world!

The fun and playful way the story addresses the relationship between taxes and social benefits was crucial for her civic education. Moreover, the lessons of ethics and citizenship present in the book served as a positive reinforcement of the values we strive to cultivate in our family.

I am very grateful that this reading has provided Camile with such important understanding from an early age. I am sure that this civic awareness will accompany her throughout her life.

Dr. Mileide Marlete Ferreira Leal Sabino
University professor, PhD in engineering and knowledge management, master's and bachelor's in administration, and mother of Camile

---

In *Tax and His Friends*, the author, a businesswoman and university professor, not only provides economic and financial knowledge didactically and pleasantly, especially for children, but also brings another contribution that I consider lacking in developing countries: a circular understanding of compulsory taxes. She shows that the resources the public power makes available for security, health, education, and infrastructure do not come from the "treasury," but from solid companies and citizens with opportunities to work and to undertake.

Almir Gorges
Former secretary of state for finance of Santa Catarina, author of the ICMS Dictionary

---

Working with the book, *Tax and His Friends*, was very rewarding from a didactic perspective for the fifth-grade children. It addresses such an important and challenging topic. With accessible and fun language, we were able to achieve our goals of making our young citizens more critical, participatory, and involved in the tax issues of society.

Larissa Pereira Sartor
Teacher, Colégio de Aplicação Univali

Besides being an extraordinary professional, her work stimulates children to understand and participate in public choices and the management of public funds. Without a doubt, it's an investment in the formation of these young citizens.

Karol Meyer
Diver, eight-time world record holder

Tax and His Friends is a delightful work that transported me to a world full of adventures, friendship, discoveries, and, above all, learning. In a novel way, Maria Claudia Hoepers addresses the topic of tax education for children in a playful and very creative manner, which certainly sparks greater interest in the subject among young readers. The narrative is light and captivating, making it impossible not to fall in love with the incredible stories of Tax and his crew. The author's initiative is admirable as tax education for children is the beginning of a necessary awareness for a seemingly complex topic. I recommend this book to everyone looking for an exciting and inspiring read!

Vanessa Camargo

Judge

With an extremely pleasant and playful text, *Tax and His Friends* brings the real possibility of educating children about taxes. It shows their relevance in terms of returns to the population (such as in health, education, and security), reinforcing important ethical lessons in a light and fun way. A beautiful "seed" planted in the new generations, for the practice of citizenship.

Dr. Marisa Luciana Schvabe de Morais

President of the Regional Council of Accounting of the State of Santa Catarina

---

With rare sensitivity, Professor Maria Claudia Hoepers presents us with a publication on tax education that is well-illustrated, fun, and accessible, aimed at the young audience. Without a doubt, this is an absolutely relevant contribution to future generations and, ultimately, to the well-being of our country.

Edson Sadao Iizuka

ANGRAD president, professor at FEI – learning and education –
social development, entrepreneurship, and enterprises

A masterpiece. A well-written book focused on taxes for children. Easy, fun, and light reading. Every child on earth should read this book. They will enjoy learning about taxes in the best possible way to make a better future for themselves.

Rodrigo K. de Mattos

Master of education, University of the Cumberlands

Copyright © 2024 Maria Claudia Hoepers
Published in the United States by Leaders Press.
www.leaderspress.com

ISBN **978-1-63735-316-5** (pbk)
ISBN **978-1-63735-317-2** (hcv)
ISBN **978-1-63735-315-8** (ebook)

Library of Congress Control Number: **2024908711**

Disclaimer

This book is provided as a source of information and education, and should not be interpreted as legal, financial, or tax advice. While the aim is to present accurate information regarding the topics discussed, laws and regulations are subject to change and can vary depending on the location. It is advised to consult a qualified professional for specific advice tailored to your situation.

The stories and characters in this book are fictional. Any resemblance to actual events, places, or people, living or dead, is purely coincidental. This book is also not intended to defame, disparage, or discredit any person or group, with all mentions made for the purpose of education and entertainment. The author and publisher assume no responsibility for any interpretations or conclusions made by the reader.

In a spirit of positivity and hope, the ultimate aim of this book is to demystify a complex and crucial topic in a light-hearted and engaging manner, aspiring to sow the seeds for a better, fairer, and more transparent future. We hope to contribute to the spread of vital knowledge among the younger generation, fostering an environment of informed and responsible citizens.

Table of Contents

Dedication

To all the children who can build a much better, fairer, and dignified future!

Acknowledgments

I would like to thank everyone who helped make this dream possible, always encouraging me never to give up! But give up? Not me! Special thanks to J. Lima, who brought the characters to life, to Candace, for her loving revision, and to my niece Carolina, who is a great source of inspiration.

About the Author

Maria Claudia Hoepers is a PhD student in economics and finance, while holding a master's degree in the same field. She is an accountant and the owner of an accounting firm in the south of Brazil. She is also a university professor with a passion for education. Growing up in a poor family, she began taking various courses at the age of twelve and has not stopped since. She has studied at some of the world's most prestigious universities, including Harvard. Her professional journey began at fourteen, and by the age of twenty-two, she had become both an entrepreneur and a university professor. Maria Claudia is a visionary who created the fiscal education project for children, *Tax and His Friends*, and cofounded a think tank focused on improving public policies. She is also actively involved in committees aimed at reducing excessive bureaucracy.

Our world is filled with beautiful landscapes, abundant natural resources, and countless opportunities. It truly is a paradise! However, to ensure that this paradise is well-maintained, with hospitals, schools, police stations, roads, and pensions operating smoothly, governments around the globe collect taxes from their citizens. Taxes are present in everything we buy and every service we use. For example, when you purchase a soccer ball, a significant portion of the price you pay consists of taxes. On average, about one-third of the price might be taxes, but this percentage can vary greatly, depending on the product and the country you live in—some countries charge less, while others charge more. But one thing is certain, taxes are everywhere: turning on a light involves paying taxes on the electricity, and you've already paid taxes on both the light bulb and the switch; opening a faucet means paying taxes on the water, and taxes have been paid on both the faucet and the fixture it's attached to. In short, it's easy to remember,

we pay taxes on everything!

Taxes play a crucial role and are one of the main sources of revenue for countries. However, many countries need to improve the management of collected resources and combat corruption, which is the misappropriation of public resources. This money belongs to us, and therefore, knowing our rights and responsibilities will certainly contribute to a better, fairer, and more transparent future, especially if this knowledge is spread from childhood.

In a fun and futuristic manner, this book aims to raise awareness among children about the significance of taxes, demonstrating simply and clearly their key role in terms of return to the population, with a focus on health, education, security, infrastructure, and other social rights, reinforcing lessons of ethics and citizenship. These lessons will be explored through the adventures of *Tax and His Friends*. Tax is responsible for distributing the taxes, and each of his five great friends is responsible for receiving a portion of these taxes and returning it to the population. They are the following:

1. Help (responsible for health)
2. Book (responsible for education)
3. Cop Pit (responsible for security)
4. Ms. Bright Bridge (responsible for infrastructure)
5. Mr. James Retired (responsible for social benefits)

Tax also counts on the help of his mother, Mother Cloud, who processes all the data and advises him when necessary. The story also features an intriguing character of dubious nature, Bad, who reminds us of the corruption and its damages. The topic is very important and quite complex, but the intention of this book is merely to clarify in a simple manner the general concepts related to the tax system and to spark interest in the discussion, especially among children, in order to contribute to reducing inequality by encouraging children's right to dream.

TAX
and his friends
BAd
Corruption
mother
CLOUD
Advisor
MR. JAMES
RETIRED
Social
Benefits
MS. BRIGHT
BRIDGE
Infrastructure
COP
BIT
Security
BOOK
Education
HELP
Health

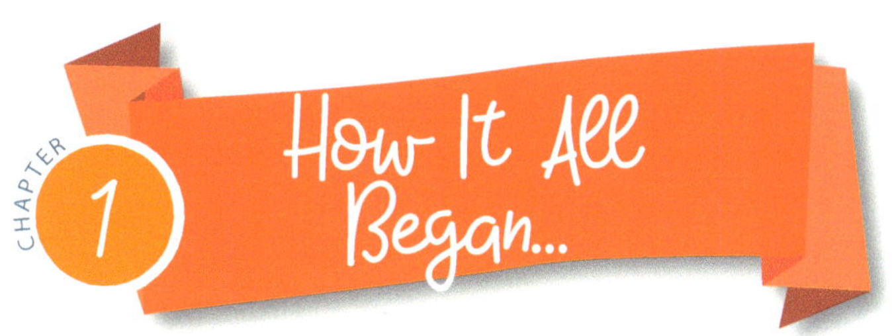

CHAPTER 1

How It All Began...

— Tax, you are a very special boy and you have a great mission!

— But, Mother Cloud, I don't know if I'm ready...

— My boy, you have just learned the first lesson of life. We can't wait until we feel ready to go after the things we want in life. That's the great beauty of life! Every day, each simple and wonderful day, is a unique opportunity to improve ourselves. We can always improve in our attitudes, our way of thinking, and acting.

— But, Mother Cloud, why me?

— You have a beautiful mission and a great responsibility. You will do a good job!

Tax is a **teenage lion** cub, but he already carries great responsibility.

Mother Cloud is Tax's mother, an extremely intelligent woman who analyzes a vast amount of information and gives her son advice whenever necessary.

— Mother Cloud, where does all this money come from?

— This money comes from taxes, and they are everywhere. Every time a person buys a product or service, about a third of the price is taxes, but in some cases, it can be half of the value or even more than that. Even from a worker's salary, a part is deducted for taxes. And all this money ends up here.

— Does this always happen? Do people have to pay taxes on everything, absolutely everything?

— Yes, my dear, people pay taxes on things like rent, water, electricity, gas, etc.

— Poor people! So much money spent on taxes! And all this money is ours?

— No, no, no, Tax, taxes are good and belong to the population. Your mission is to divide it correctly so that it returns to its true owners to help them with health, education, security, infrastructure, and social benefits.

— But if the money belongs to the people and should return to them, wouldn't it be easier to simply not charge taxes and let everyone take care of themselves?

— Ha! Ha! Ha! Of course not, young man! Can you imagine being responsible for everything on your own?! Taking care of your health, education, security, building roads, etc. would be a lot of work!

Tax realizes that taxes play an important role and that it would be impossible to take care of everything alone.

Tax has five great friends, who also have a huge responsibility. They receive a portion of the taxes weekly and need to distribute it to the population. Each friend is responsible for a specific area.

Help is responsible for health.

Book is responsible for education.

Cop Pit is responsible for security.

Ms. Bright Bridge is responsible for infrastructure.

Mr. James Retired is responsible for social benefits.

Tax is responsible for dividing the total amount of taxes and distributing it to his friends, a relatively simple task that cannot afford mistakes, as it would be devastating!

It's easy for Tax to remember that the division is by five; after all, there are five friends. They are inseparable, loyal, and sincere.

After dividing, Tax sends an equal part to each friend with the following message: "Dear friend, use this money with responsibility, wisdom, and honesty."

Thus, each friend receives weekly a fifth of the total amount collected from taxes.

Help always responds with great joy: "Thank you, my friend! You can always count on me! I will use a part of this money to improve health, the most important thing! Another part will go to disease prevention programs, and the largest portion will be allocated to innovation."

Book, almost always moved, cries with joy!

Once he calms down, he also responds: "Tax, my friend, education transforms lives, and I will use this money with great wisdom to improve as many lives as possible. I will invest in financial education, lessons on ethics, citizenship, and robotics. Through education, we can reduce inequality and create equal opportunities for everyone."

Book is truly passionate about the transformative power of education.

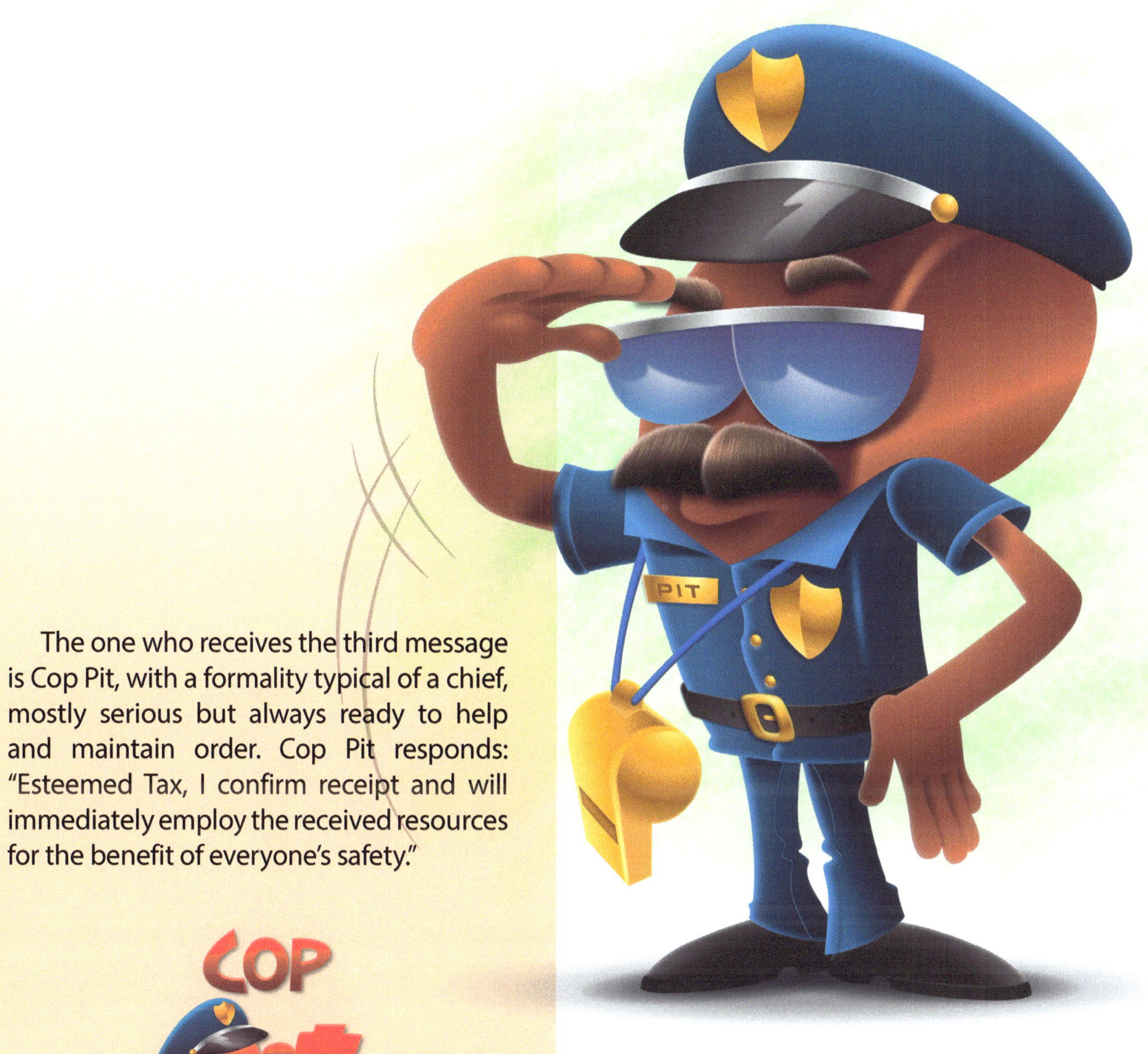

The one who receives the third message is Cop Pit, with a formality typical of a chief, mostly serious but always ready to help and maintain order. Cop Pit responds: "Esteemed Tax, I confirm receipt and will immediately employ the received resources for the benefit of everyone's safety."

MS. BRIGHT BRIDGE

With a calm voice, now a bit gravelly but full of wisdom, the next to respond is Ms. Bright Bridge, who has admirable life experience.

"Dear Tax, with all my love, I will use the money for some preventive repairs and also to research new technologies. This old lady here has an open mind, my dear! A big hug and much light on your path!"

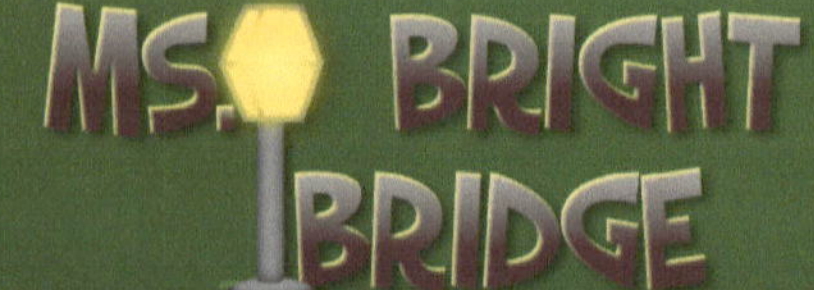

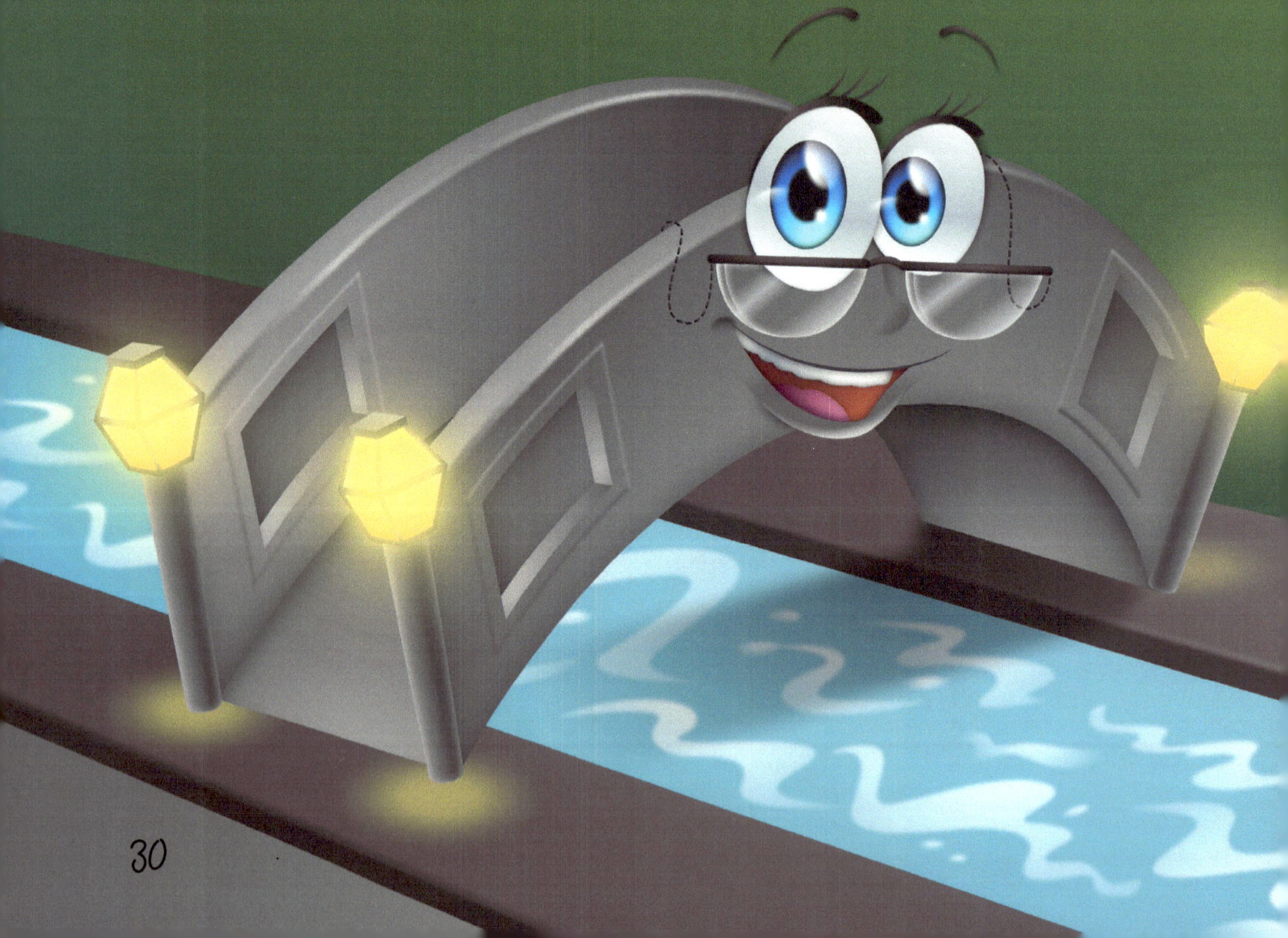

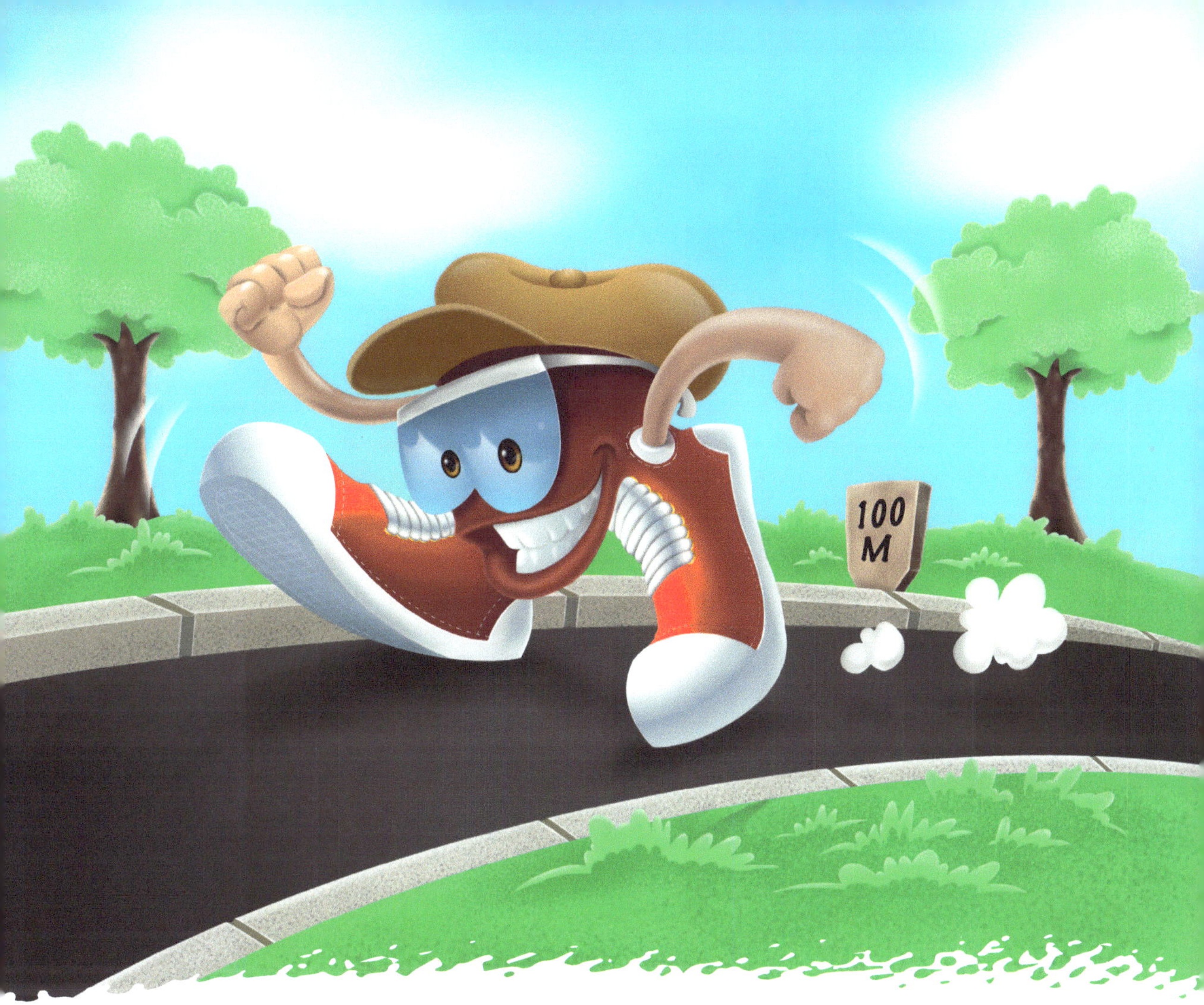

Lastly, we have Mr. James Retired. He is a charming old man who dedicated his life to work, and if you think today he's tired and sitting in his rocking chair because of this, you are mistaken! Mr. James is an athlete who inspires the youth to engage in sports and to eat healthily. At eighty years old, he has energy, vitality, and contagious joy!

Mr. James Retired responds: "Thank you very much, buddy! I'm going to share what I received with the young people of my age. I worked hard during my life and at this moment I can enjoy a bit more. This money helps a lot! Now, I'm off to run because I have a marathon coming up."

Taxes Are Good, and the System Works

For a long time, everything was going well... The population was healthy, including a significant reduction in the number of medications sold as a result of the disease prevention program, a major initiative by Help.

Productivity greatly increased, and people were able to work fewer hours a day, dedicating a good portion of their time to studies and family. Book invested in various programs, including robotics, artificial intelligence, meditation (an idea from Ms. Bright Bridge that he never ceases to thank her for), and various others.

Cop Pit is proud to have gone exactly one thousand days without any police incidents. People walk the streets without fear, sometimes even texting on their cellphones. He even warns them, as they might bump into each other!

The handbag industry has changed, and now there are no more zippers because the bags are left open! After all, no one thinks about touching something that isn't theirs!

Ah! I almost forgot! There have been so many changes in recent years... The industry for fences and locks had to adapt, as these products are no longer used.

There are no more walls around houses, and the landscape has become beautiful.

Streets and avenues are illuminated, but with awareness, not wasting energy, always taking advantage of solar light. It's all thanks to Ms. Bright Bridge, who is always humming a tune.

Rivers, lakes, and ponds are all sparkling clean! The water is so clear that you can even drink it and see the little fish showing off.

Potholes in the roads?! We've been eight hundred days without a single one! The last case recorded still stirs controversy, as it was the size of a pinhead. Someone noticed and took a photo at the exact moment a little ant fell backwards into the hole... It made the front page of every newspaper, and for weeks, that was all anyone talked about. The headline was: "National Shame! A pothole appears on a road in the south." Oh, and the little ant is doing just fine!

Retirees over seventy are happy. They are examples of vitality, engaging in sports, meditation, singing, dancing, and even dedicating one day a week to teaching younger people in the program "The Voice of Experience", an idea from Book that Mr. James Retired embraced readily. In fact, the day of the live session is the most anticipated moment for the youth, as the lessons are truly valuable.

Tax lives very happily, and even though everything is working, everyone always wants to improve more and more...

As usual, Tax has the most important mission, ensuring the correct distribution of money, dividing it by five.

Normally, the total amount to be divided is $50 billion per week, but in more difficult periods it dropped to $40 billion, and in better times, it reached $60 billion.

Tax is very smart, but also very lucky, as historically the total amount of taxes has always been a multiple of five, which greatly simplifies the calculation.

Tax can even do the math blindfolded, because he is so accustomed to doing this division.

CHAPTER 3

Taxes Are Good, but Sometimes the System Doesn't Work

One fine day, Tax receives $48 billion to distribute. Distracted, he quickly concludes:

- $12 billion for Help;
- $12 billion for Book;
- $12 billion for Cop Pit;
- $12 billion for Ms. Bright Bridge.

And when he goes to transfer to Mr. James Retired... Where's the money?! Tax doesn't understand what happened! He has been doing this without making any mistakes for years!

In tears, he calls Mother Cloud:

— Mother Cloud, help me! I made a mistake! I got the division wrong!

— My dear, what happened?

— It wasn't a multiple of five! I got confused, and now I have nothing for Mr. James Retired, nothing at all! What do I do now?

— My dear, didn't you check? I always taught you to check your calculations because your work is very important.

— Mother Cloud, I failed! I always got the calculation right, so for a few months, I stopped checking, because it always, always worked out!

— Let's learn from our mistakes dear. This is why we need to check our calculations every time. When it comes to numbers, verification is just as important as the calculation itself.

— What do I do now Mother Cloud?

— Call your friends and ask them to send the money back, so you can try to reverse the situation!

Tax calls Help.

— Help, I need help!

— Of course, my friend, how can I help you?

— I made a mistake in the division; I need you to return part of the amount.

— Impossible!

— Why?

— I've already allocated everything! I'm very quick! We're investing in disease prevention and promoting healthy habits. I've invested it all, and my team is waiting for next week's resources to proceed with the studies. Health is no joking matter!

— Ok, thanks! I'll try with Book...

Tax then calls Book:

— Hello, Book!

— Hello, great, Tax!

— I made a mistake in the division; I need you to return part of the amount.

— I would love to help you, but unfortunately, that won't be possible.

— Why?

— I've already created more courses, and the money has been fully used.

— But, all of it?

— "If you think education is expensive, try ignorance," as a great educator once said.

— Beautiful words, Book, great quote!

— I love quotes! They enrich the argument.

— Ok! I'm glad you've invested well.

— Have a great day, my friend! Ah! Try Cop Pit!

Tax, still hoping to solve the problem, calls Cop Pit.

— Hello, Cop Pit!

— Always at your service, Tax! How can I assist you?

— I made a mistake in the division; I need you to return part of the amount.

— Dear friend, I was tasked with allocating the resources for security, and I have always done so promptly, responsibly, and efficiently. Thus, I no longer have this week's resources. We've already updated our apps and mapped one hundred percent of the population. Our new identification system is now operational in maternity wards. Today, fingerprint collection, DNA sampling, and facial recognition are conducted simultaneously with the newborn screening test. And we are studying to implement these in the prenatal exam, as early as the third month of pregnancy.

— So, you used the extra resource for facial recognition of newborns... Why? – Tax asks.

— Because, this way, our systems can, for example, project with 98 percent accuracy the facial recognition of an adult, extracted from the baby's record, helping to solve cases of missing children. Moreover, with DNA collection, we've made significant advances in analyzing compatibility for organ donation. With all pride and respect, Tax, my team is top-notch! – Cop Pit proudly explains.

— Good job! I'll turn to Ms. Bright Bridge.

—Hello, Ms. Bright Bridge! How are you?

—Lovely, Tax, I am doing very well! We just finished adapting the remaining highways to safely accommodate autonomous vehicles, those that move without a driver! In addition, 100 percent of the roads and public spaces now operate on solar energy. Isn't it magnificent?! Our system is foolproof!

—I thought it was!

—Was? Why?

—I made a mistake, a serious mistake! I got the division of money wrong and now I have nothing, absolutely nothing, to pass on to Mr. James Retired.

—I'm sorry, dear, but I can't help you! Try talking to Mr. James Retired. Be honest with him about what happened.

Very sad, with his head down and feeling ashamed, Tax calls Mr. James Retired.

— I'm sorry to bother you, Mr. James Retired, but I don't bring good news...

— What happened, Tax? You're scaring me!

— I made a mistake, a serious mistake, my fault... And I can't pay you anything this week.

— What do you mean, Tax? What now?

— Sorry!

— Tax, we, the retirees, have worked our entire lives and contributed a lot. We need this money for our survival. We need to eat, pay rent, and many other things... This has never happened before!

— I'm so sorry!

— Tax, but why don't you think of another solution?! I have experience, I can help you. Instead of cutting 100 percent of my resources, why not take a little from each?

— I tried, but they've already used everything!

— What a disappointment, Tax! I thought you considered all five of us important, but it seems I'm no longer so useful…

— Please, Mr. James Retired, don't think that! It was a mistake!

— Mistakes cost dearly and can bring pain and suffering. I understand you didn't mean any harm, but now I need to inform everyone about the benefit cut.

Tax ends the call and then is overwhelmed by sadness.

CHAPTER 4

Mismanagement of Taxes Leads to Chaos

Mr. James Retired informs all the retirees that they are out of money.

While some, like Mr. James Retired, tie their shoelaces and go looking for jobs, which are hard to find...

Others fall ill and end up in the hospital. The chaos in healthcare makes Help stop various investments in technology to be able to buy medicine.

A group of daring elderly people stormed one of the few remaining bank branches. True, I forgot to mention! With the regulation of cryptocurrencies, there's no more paper money, it's all electronic now! That's why there are hardly any bank branches left!

With the storming of the bank branch, Cop Pit was called to report the incident and take the little thieves away, the youngest of whom was ninety-three years old.

The problem is that since there hadn't been a recorded incident in so long, the old prisons had been transformed. Exactly half of them were adapted for study and development of robotics, a quarter was allocated for recycling materials, and the remainder for organic farming.

In addition to everything, there was a large protest by the retirees, who blocked the bridge, stopping all traffic. Some, "accidentally," got carried away and threw stones, damaging dozens of solar panels.

At this moment, very worried, Ms. Bright Bridge tries to calm everyone down:

— Gentlemen, let's keep calm. "To lose patience is to lose the battle," as a great man once said.

Shortly after, Cop Pit and his troops manage to disperse the crowd.

Alone in the dark, Ms. Bright Bridge
cries, full of marks and scars.

The next day, not only Mr. James Retired but also Help, Ms. Bright Bridge, and Cop Pit try desperately to speak with Tax, as they urgently need help.

Tax turns to Book and tells him about the severity of the situation.

Book, who is already emotional by nature, cries nonstop, and his tears flood the academic world, preventing students from studying.

Tax is devastated and turns to his mother for advice.

Mother Cloud, always wise, seems to always have a solution for everything.

— Dear, advise everyone to use their emergency reserves until everything returns to normal, as the situation is serious!

— Great idea, Mother Cloud! Where would I be without you?!

— Dear, I hope I've helped, but be quick. I'm checking here that there's been a decrease in the total collected for next week. Without money, all the retirees have stopped spending, and if you don't act quickly, the problem could get worse.

Tax calls everyone to discuss the release of the emergency reserve.

Book, still crying, starts to speak.

—I think we have a little problem... Since we hadn't had any emergencies for a long time, I decided to use the reserve, which was just sitting there doing nothing, to change the covers of the books. They look beautiful now!

—Book, emergency reserves are not for that!

—Sorry, Tax, but I put new covers on them, in a blueberry color, and they look wonderful. I love blue, I love blueberries, so they're perfect!

52

Ms. Bright Bridge asks to speak and informs that she has already used the emergency reserve to repair the solar panels, which were damaged during the retirees' protest.

Tax questions Help:

— What about you?

— We didn't have medication stocks because the population wasn't getting sick anymore. However, with the lack of money from the retirees, many fell ill, and I had to use the reserve to buy medicine. Now the situation is under control.

At this moment, all eyes turn to Cop Pit. Still crying, Book begins to speak:

— Cop Pit, you are our hope! Do you have your emergency reserve?

Cop Pit puffs out his chest, takes a deep breath, and salutes Tax firmly:

— Mission given is mission accomplished! I have the intact amount, gentlemen, and although it's stated in the rulebook that this reserve can only be used within my own department, I understand the situation is chaotic. So, I'll be happy to help you!

Everyone breathes a sigh of relief. Tax walks towards Cop Pit and gives him a big, warm hug and says, "Thank you."

Cop Pit immediately divides the money from his emergency reserve into two parts, prioritizing the areas in the most delicate situation, in this order: Mr. James Retired and Help.

Cop Pit's reserve is enough to solve the problem.

Everyone expresses their gratitude, and some comments start to arise. Among them, Help says:

—Sorry, but I believe we need someone with more experience to handle the tax division.

At this moment, Tax can't hide his sadness and disappointment with himself.

Weeks go by, and Tax continues to make his divisions, now with more care and always double-checking them thoroughly. However, he still shows signs of carrying the weight of the mistake. Tax truly seems unable to forgive himself.

Months pass, and everything seems to flow smoothly. Tax ends up distancing himself a bit from his friends, but he never fails to fulfill his mission.

CHAPTER 5

The Beginning of Corruption

One day, someone very cheerful appears and quickly introduces himself.

— Hello! You must be Tax, the big guy who took on the responsibility of dividing the money, right?

His eyes sparkle strangely when he says the word "money."

— Yes, it's me, responsible and irresponsible sometimes. And you, who are you? – Tax asks.

— Nice to meet you, I'm Bad!

— Bad?! Bad, the Bad? – Tax repeats, scared.

— Yes, it's me, the generous, reliable, and unforgettable Bad.

— Mother Cloud always told me to stay away from you!

— But what have I done to you, Tax?

— Sorry, you haven't done anything to me. I'm just upset with myself.

— Upset, why? Let me help! We can be friends… inseparable friends! And we can take care of the money together – grumbles Bad.

— What did you say?

— Nothing, nothing, just that I would love to be your friend. But tell me, why are you sad? Problems with your mane?

— My mane? What's wrong with my mane?

— Nothing, forget it!

— Speak, please! – Tax insists.

— Well… Someone with such responsibility would need a powerful mane.

— I thought so too. I talked to Mother Cloud, and she said to be patient, everything has its time. When I grow up, I'll have a beautiful mane.

Tax closes his eyes and imagines himself with his exuberant mane.

— Mothers never want to hurt us! – exclaims Bad. — But why wait?

— Bad, manes aren't sold in supermarkets.

— It's just sad to see a grown lion throw away his mane.

— But what are you talking about?

—Well, I know a Buddhist lion who will cut his mane to live in a distant place, a monastery, to pray and help his community. Anyways, he's just looking for a good lion to buy it because he intends to use the money for humanitarian causes.

Tax, touched, responds:

— I would love to have an impressive mane. I would love even more to be able to contribute to such a noble cause, but...

— But what? You have access to a fortune every week, only you know the total value. Be smart! If you take just a small amount from each one, no one will notice.

— Of course not, Bad! That's not right!

— Think about it! Think about humanitarian causes! Think about how much happier you'll be, and happy people are much more productive.

Tax, confused with so much information, doesn't seem to find the idea so bad.

Bad continues to argue:

— Don't think about the fact that you're buying the mane, but rather helping in humanitarian causes. The mane is just an act of kindness from the Buddhist lion to you.

— Yeah, thinking like that... will these humanitarian causes impact many lives? – questions Tax.

Bad, already impatient, rushes to answer:

— Yes, trillions of people.

— What do you mean? The world population is just over seven billion.

— Oh, I think I got confused with that detail! So, are you going to help or not? I guarantee it's a noble cause!

Tax, still confused, decides to accept Bad's proposal.

Bad walks away from Tax muttering to himself:

That naive lion... he believed that story! There's no Buddhist lion at all. I'll just buy some synthetic hair for a few crumbs and keep all the money for myself. I'm the kind who loves doing good! I always love doing good for myself!

The next day, Bad returns, receives the amount, hands over the synthetic mane to Tax, and then quickly leaves. He said he needed to collect more contributions for humanitarian causes.

Tax calls Mother Cloud to share the good deed he just did and to show off his mane.

Within seconds, due to her vast wisdom, Mother Cloud realizes that Tax fell for a scam.

And when Tax reveals the name of his newest "friend," Mother Cloud is disappointed.

— I had already warned you to stay away from Bad! He's corrupt!

— But, Mother Cloud, he seemed to be my friend.

— You were deceived!

At that moment, Tax removes the synthetic mane and cries, feeling very guilty.

So sad, Tax ends up in the hospital.

Since medicine has advanced so much, when someone goes to the hospital, it ends up being front-page news, as cases of illness are rare, since almost everything is resolved with preventive medicine.

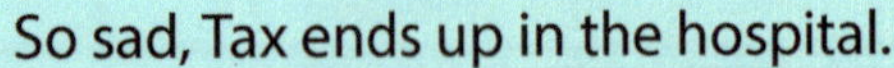

Bad sees the headline on a newspaper and thinks, "This is my chance! You're done for, Tax!"

Bad approaches Tax and starts his speech:

— My friend, Tax, your mistake caused a lot of harm!

— Bad, do you still have the audacity to call me a friend? You tricked me, causing me to make mistakes!

— It was just a test, but you're too young for this mission. You don't even seem like a lion! You act like a cat! You're a disgrace! Always making mistakes and believing in any story... Get out of here! I can do your job much better!

— Bad, this mission is mine!

— You're nothing but a useless teenager who can't even do a simple division. Go away, Tax, everyone will be better off without you around!

Sad and feeling guilty for everything,
Tax walks away and leaves.

CHAPTER 6

When Corruption Takes Over

Bad calls together all five friends for a meeting and begins his speech:

— Dear friends, I have important news for everyone: Tax has given up the mission of being responsible for the division of taxes and has left.

— How so? – they ask.

— I insisted that he stay, told him I could help, but he didn't want to listen to me and left.

— What do we do now? – they ask, worried.

— Well, now comes the good part... I will be the new person in charge of the tax division and I will do an excellent job.

Everyone looks unsure, but still surprised by Tax's departure, they end up saying nothing and Bad takes over.

Meanwhile, Mother Cloud tries to talk to Tax, but can't find him.

She decides then to confront Bad:

— Bad, you're not welcome here!

— Wow! Always so kind! I'm only here because everyone asked.

Mother Cloud seems not to believe him, but she's so worried about Tax that she ends up accepting Bad.

Tax continues his journey all alone, still feeling guilty about everything.

Time passes, and Mother Cloud keeps searching for Tax.

Bad starts his job and is already planning a big change.

— Divide by five, only after I take half for myself. I really love doing good, but only for myself!

Bad then begins to take half of the money for himself and divides the other half. He uses the money that he keeps for himself to buy jewelry, cars, and throw big parties.

Meanwhile, the population suffers because they are receiving only half of the tax money. Therefore, they spend only on what is urgent, leaving no more money for numerous prevention programs.

With an elaborate plan, Bad brings everyone together to announce some news:

— Dear boys and girls, I bring good news!

— Bad, we're having a lot of problems! Healthcare is in chaos! – says Help.

— We're going to invest in a big construction. – Bad states.

— That's good news, Bad! Will it be a new hospital? We really need it!

— Not exactly. In fact, we're going to build a very luxurious mansion, which will be my new home.

— Bad, that's not fair! – everyone shouts.

— But I have an idea! I think we spend too much on education, and we're going to cut it by 100 percent, so we'll have more money for other areas.

Book doesn't agree, of course, but as everyone is really in need of money, they end up thinking only of their own areas.

Book questions Bad:

— Bad, why cut 100 percent of the money for education? That's a mistake!

Bad moves closer to Book and speaks in a low voice:

— Uneducated people are like puppets in the hands of the clever.

Book, saddened, continues to cry, about to drown in his own tears.

Bad's changes don't stop there... He launches a program to encourage people to eat only fast food. As a result, the population becomes increasingly ill.

He stops investing in basic sanitation and encourages everyone to pollute the rivers, dirtying the water and causing a bad smell in the cities.

Bad also spreads his evil through fake news, claiming that vaccines are poisons to humanity. Thus, people stopped getting vaccinated, and diseases that were no longer heard of came back with full force.

At the same time, Bad continues with his parties...

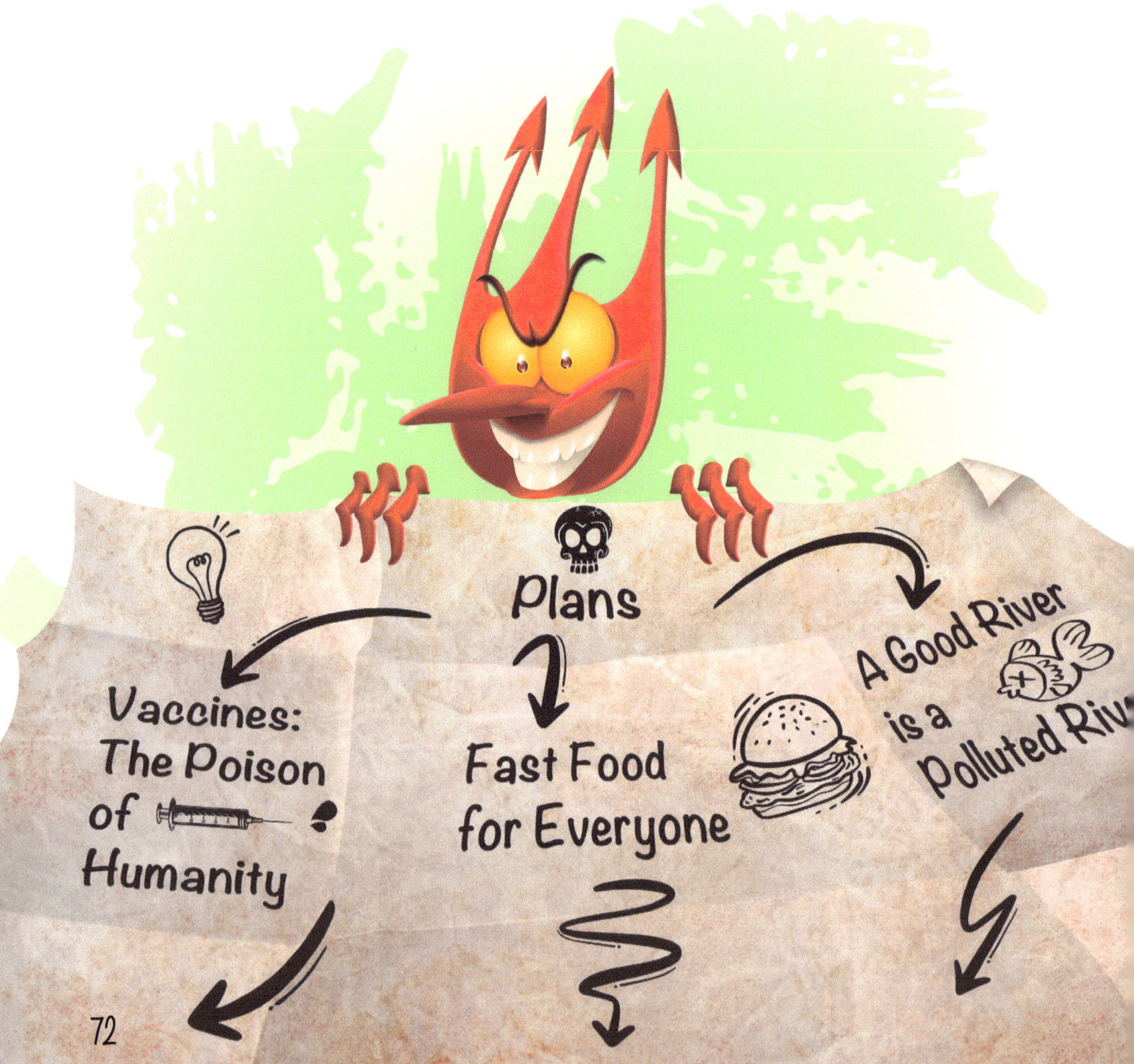

7 There Is Still Hope

Far away, Mother Cloud, like any good mother, never gives up looking for Tax. One beautiful day, she finds him and asks him to come with her to the mountains, to teach him a lesson she learned from her grandfather:

— Tax, how are you? – Mother Cloud asks.

— Sad.

The place, in the mountains, produces an extraordinary echo, repeating the word "sad" several times.

— What have you been doing all this time? – Mother Cloud questions.

— Nothing, I do everything wrong.

Again and frighteningly, the words "Nothing, I do everything wrong" are echoed.

Tax continues:

— Why did you bring me here, Mother Cloud?

— Dear, my grandfather taught me that life is like an echo. So be careful what you're putting out into the world, because it will come right back to you!

— Mother Cloud, I think I understand everything now!

Tax runs off, and Mother Cloud looks worried.

— Where are you going dear?

— I need to make up for lost time.

Tax, in a hurry, buys several math books to study and improve his calculations, then continues his search for his friends.

The situation is dire: everyone is out of money and without hope.

Deciding to take action, Tax invades Bad's mansion.

— Bad, where are you?

— Hello! What a pleasant surprise, my friend. How can I assist you?

— Leave, Bad, you're corrupt. This mansion isn't yours!

— Calm down, friend. How about I offer you a small room in this mansion? We could be partners.

— Never! Trust can't be bought, it must be earned, and I no longer trust you! Leave now!

Tax appears to have learned from his past mistakes and is now full of self-confidence, determined to reclaim his role and help everyone!

The friends find Tax in the mansion and are very happy about his return.

Bad moves away from the crowd and tries to escape, when suddenly Cop Pit approaches him:

— Bad, you corrupt man! I'm going to take you to where you belong. I am taking you right to jail!

— Oh, Cop Pit, you're always so charming. May I offer you some jewelry? They would match your whistle.

—I'll take and sell the jewelry to return the money to its rightful owners, the people. And I hope you never get out of jail.

In no time, with Tax back in charge of distributing the taxes, everything returns to normal.

Tax is full of great ideas, and innovation is everywhere, with autonomous vehicles, artificial intelligence, the Internet of Things, etc. Everyone is happy and engaged in improving everything for the good of all.

Ms. Bright Bridge is responsible for setting up the autonomous vehicles.

Book uses one of the vehicles to go shopping and comes back with many complaints.

— Excuse me, but I think a young person could do this job with more quality. The car you programmed stopped at the farthest parking spot from the supermarket door, exactly the opposite of what I always do. I think this system has malfunctioned!

Patiently, with a wisdom that is only acquired with experience, Ms. Bright Bridge replies:

— Dear and healthy Book, I configured the vehicles so that, through sensory recognition, the closest spots are reserved for those in need. In fact, this was already practiced by kind people, long before autonomous cars became a reality.

Book, embarrassed, says:

— I'm ashamed, I really had never thought of it that way. I will change my attitude and take the opportunity to inspire others as well. I will include important new topics like keeping the left side of escalators free for those who want to walk faster and I will suggest the creation of the Olympics of Kindness and Gentleness. It will be a success with everyone being kind and gentle.

Ms. Bright Bridge smiles happily.

Tax addresses everyone and says:

— Dear friends! We have been through many troubles, mistakes were made, and the population, the true owners of the money, suffered the most. I have been studying a lot, always seeking to improve, and I propose we rewrite the rules with CARE, so that everyone understands their rights and duties.

Cop Pit comments:

— With all due respect, friend, with or without care, I just want the rules to be clear and for everyone to be able to follow them.

— That's exactly what I'm proposing, "CARE" stands for:

Clear
Alerts, with
Responsability, and
Empathy

— If the rules are written with CARE, everyone will understand.

— Wow! – exclaims Book!

Tax continues his speech:

— I would like to announce that this will be my last year leading the tax division. I've been studying a lot and believe that renewal is important. Moreover, I think it's good to establish some rules for whoever wants to take on the mission. I believe the most important of these should be the implementation of an aptitude test to verify if the person has the capability to manage the taxes well, and also, an annual performance review to check if the work is being done properly.

Cop Pit asks to speak:

— What a sublime idea! I think these rules should be applied to all of us!

Ms. Bright Bridge also agrees and addresses Book:

— Dear Book, I have some contributions to make. I think you waste a lot of time on some topics that don't make much sense today, like teaching handwriting in a one hundred percent digital environment. I believe you could replace these classes with reinforcement in mathematics, financial education, or data analysis. What do you think?

— I love handwriting, especially when it is written in blueberry blue, but you are right! Any other suggestions?

— Since you asked... I do! – says Ms. Bright Bridge. You spend days, weeks, and even months reading nonstop, but what's the point?

— I have a lot of knowledge and that's transformative! – responds Book.

— I agree!

—Then, I'm sorry, what you're saying doesn't make sense!

— What good is so much knowledge locked in a box?! It's only transforming yourself and that doesn't bring happiness! Now try opening your box and sharing... That way, not only will your life be transformed, but everyone around you will be too. – explains Ms. Bright Bridge.

— I'm moved, as soon as the tears dry, I'll share everything I know, everything, all of it.

CHAPTER 8

The Story Doesn't End

And they all lived happily ever after?

No, no, no! Many mistakes were made. Believe me, many! Some learned and evolved from their mistakes, while others did not. A lot of confusion came after all of this, and unexpected situations brought disorder. Controversies arose and wrong decisions were made. Many of these wrong decisions were made due to not focusing on what is truly important. Sometimes people focus on something so small when there is a huge problem to solve. It's as if there was an elephant in the room, but no one can see it because they're focused on an ant. This is just a metaphor, but believe me, if I were to count all the times that mistakes were made due to not focusing on what really matters (laughs), that would fill another book.

As time went by, the concept of a smart city was created. They began to be governed by the help of artificial intelligence and no longer just by passionate leaders. Algorithms (calculations and logical procedures for problem-solving) are being developed to assist in unbiased decision-making, which is based on data and not just intuition. Believe me, most of the time, our intuition ends up tricking us.

Still, we should not disregard intuition, as it represents the voice that comes from the heart and makes us act with love, kindness, and gentleness, as if we were protected and guided by a true Mother Cloud.

Stay informed!

Most countries provide information about the revenue of the country, its state, or its municipality. Look for official sites and sources. Make sure to stay updated!

It's important to remember that this money is ours and needs to be treated with care, responsibility, and transparency! We need to know if it's being used correctly, for the benefit of the population, through investments in health, education, security, infrastructure, and social benefits.

We can live in a better, fairer, and more dignified country for everyone!

And you, who are now reading this book, know that the world will be a better place because YOU are a part of it!

Visit our website:
www.taxandhisfriends.com
and/or contact us:
contact@taxandhisfriends.com

If you liked the project, we invite you to check out and follow our social media @taxandhisfriends.

And, of course, if you can help share this idea, we would be deeply honored!

www.ingramcontent.com/pod-product-compliance
Lightning Source LLC
Chambersburg PA
CBHW041129100726
47911CB00002B/75